This edition published by Parragon Books Ltd in 2015 and distributed by

Parragon Inc.
440 Park Avenue South, 13th Floor
New York, NY 10016
www.parragon.com

ISBN 978-1-4723-6710-5

Printed in China

The Three Musketeers

Bath · New York · Cologne · Melbourne · Delhi
Hong Kong · Shenzhen · Singapore · Amsterdam

Starring:

Mickey Mouse

Donald Duck

Goofy

Clarabelle

Captain Pete

Minnie Mouse

Daisy Duck

Pluto

Once upon a time, there lived three young friends named Mickey, Donald, and Goofy. The friends dreamed of being like their greatest heroes—the Musketeers. The Musketeers were the strongest, bravest, cleverest soldiers in France. And they lived by these words: All for one and one for all!

Mickey and his friends were willing to do anything to become Musketeers. They even worked at the Musketeers' headquarters. They hoped that Captain Pete, head of the Musketeers, would notice them.

But Captain Pete had plans of his own—evil plans. Pete wanted to become king of France!

Captain Pete hired the Beagle Boys to kidnap Princess Minnie. Once the princess was out of the way, Pete could claim the throne.

Princess Minnie was having tea with Lady Daisy one day. As she went out to the garden, the Beagle Boys pushed a safe off the balcony. They just missed the princess!

When Captain Pete found out what had happened, he was furious!
"I didn't say 'drop a safe,' I said, 'keep her safe!'"

Pete turned to his lieutenant, Clarabelle. "Throw these clowns
into the pit!"

After she had taken the Beagle Boys to the pit, Clarabelle received a phone call from a very upset Princess Minnie. She demanded to see Captain Pete immediately!

"I want bodyguards," Princess Minnie told Pete. "Musketeer bodyguards!"
She didn't realize that it was Captain Pete's helpers who had nearly dropped
the safe on her!

Pete knew that real Musketeers would interfere with his plan.
Luckily, he had an idea. "I've got just the men for you, Princess!"

Pete marched out to the courtyard. "You three are going to be Musketeers!" he told Mickey, Goofy, and Donald. They were delighted.

Later that day, the three new Musketeers were escorting
Princess Minnie and Lady Daisy on a trip through the countryside.
But Captain Pete had sent the Beagle Boys after Minnie again.

As the royal coach passed by their hiding place in a tree, the Beagle Boys jumped onto it. Mickey and Goofy were ready to fight, but Donald was scared and jumped into the coach.

"Get back out there, you coward," Minnie scolded.

Defeated by the Beagle Boys, all three of the Musketeers ended up in the mud. The Beagle Boys made their escape in the royal coach, with Princess Minnie and Lady Daisy still inside!

But Mickey wasn't ready to give up. "Pete made us Musketeers, remember? That means it's our job to save the princess!"

After a long walk,
the Musketeers found the
empty royal coach near a tower.
But when Mickey tried to open
the tower door, it was stuck.

"Let me give it a try,"
Goofy said. He ran at the door
as hard as he could. It swung
open, and he raced inside.

As Goofy ran up the stairs of the tower, he accidentally knocked things out the window. That gave him an idea!

Goofy knocked the Beagle Boys
out of the window, too! Then he told
Princess Minnie and Lady Daisy that
he was there to rescue them.

The Three Musketeers took Princess Minnie and Lady Daisy back to the royal castle. As Goofy stood guard outside Princess Minnie's room, he saw Mickey's shadow. "Help me, Musketeer Goofy," a voice said.

Goofy followed the shadow out of the palace. But it wasn't Mickey at all—Clarabelle had tricked Goofy! She quickly captured him.

Meanwhile, the Beagle Boys had found Donald and Pluto. Pluto ran away, and Donald dived inside a suit of armor and hid. The Beagle Boys walked past Donald without even seeing him.

Before long, Mickey found Donald inside the suit of armor. Donald told Mickey that he had heard the Beagle Boys talking about their boss—Captain Pete!

Mickey was shocked. Pete was the bad guy! Mickey went to find Captain Pete.

But Captain Pete found him first. He locked Mickey in a cage and carried him to a remote island prison....

Pete chained Mickey to a wall deep in the prison dungeons.

"Looks like this is the end of the line," Pete said.

"My pals will be right behind us," Mickey replied.

"Oh, sure," Pete said. "Face it! You're on your own!"

Suddenly, water began to pour into the dungeon. Soon it would be flooded!

"See you later, Mickey," Captain Pete laughed as he walked out.

Mickey wasn't the only Musketeer in danger. Clarabelle was about to throw Goofy off a bridge! But suddenly, as she bragged about Pete's plans for Mickey, the bridge gave way. Clarabelle and Goofy plunged over the side, right into a boat that was being rowed by Donald!

Goofy knew that they had to save Mickey. "It's all for one and one for all," he said. Donald was scared, but he agreed to help.

The water in Mickey's cell was rising. He hadn't been able to break free from his chains. Then, just when it looked as if all hope was lost, Goofy and Donald arrived! They quickly freed Mickey and got him to safety.

The Three Musketeers raced off to save the princess.

Meanwhile, at the opera, Pete put Lady Daisy and Princess Minnie in a large sack and gave it to two of the Beagle Boys!

The smallest Beagle Boy, dressed as Princess Minnie, stepped onstage. "My loyal subjects," the fake princess said. "I now present your new ruler— King Pete!"

Luckily, Donald, Mickey, and Goofy arrived to save the day!

Mickey quickly freed Minnie and Daisy,
then Captain Pete jumped onstage!
"It's all over," Pete said.
"Wanna bet?" Mickey said.
Together, Mickey, Goofy, and Donald
defeated Captain Pete and ended his evil plan.

And that is how Princess Minnie came to make all three friends her official Royal Musketeers!

Mickey, Donald, and Goofy could hardly believe it. They might not be the biggest, bravest, or smartest of all, but by working together, they had made their dreams come true.

As the crowd cheered, Mickey couldn't help shouting, "All for one . . ."

And everyone—even Princess Minnie—cheered, "And one for all!"

The End